MY 1ST GRAPHIC NOVEL®

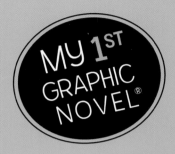

CLUES IN THE ATTIC

MY FIRST GRAPHIC NOVELS ARE PUBLISHED BY STONE ARCH BOOKS
A CAPSTONE IMPRINT
151 GOOD COUNSEL DRIVE, P.O. BOX 669
MANKATO, MINNESOTA 56002
WWW.CAPSTONEPUB.COM

Library of Congress Cataloging-in-Publication data is available on the
Library of Congress website.

Library Binding: 978-1-4342-1889-6
Paperback: 978-1-4342-2283-1

Summary: Ben lost something that belongs to his sister, and he has to find it.
Even though he's scared, he has to go into the attic to find what's missing.

Art Director: BOB LENTZ
Graphic Designer: EMILY HARRIS
Production Specialist: MICHELLE BIEDSCHEID

CLUES
IN THE ATTIC

by Cari Meister

illustrated by Rémy Simard

STONE ARCH BOOKS
a capstone imprint

HOW TO READ A GRAPHIC NOVEL

Graphic novels are easy to read. Boxes called panels show you how to follow the story. Look at the panels from left to right and top to bottom.

Read the word boxes and word balloons from left to right as well. Don't forget the sound and action words in the pictures.

The pictures and the words work together to tell the whole story.

Ben climbed the stairs. He opened the attic door.
He was glad his sister, Sofia, did not see him.

The attic was dark. The attic was cold. The attic was scary.

Ben turned on the light. The light blinked once.
Then it went dark.

The attic smelled funny. There were strange noises.
There were strange shapes.

Ben wanted to leave. But he couldn't. He was looking for something.

Suddenly, the door slammed shut.

Ben opened the door and ran down the stairs.

He tripped. He fell.

Sofia heard the noises. She found Ben at the bottom of the attic stairs.

After dinner, Ben decided to go back to the attic. But first he needed his flashlight.

The stairs creaked under his feet.

There were cobwebs everywhere! There were also strange noises. It didn't matter. Ben had to be brave.

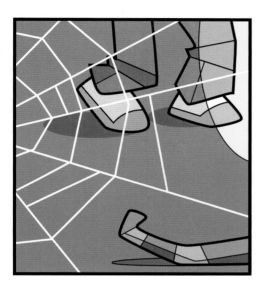

That's when Ben saw something move.

Ben slammed the attic door and ran.

Sofia was waiting at the bottom of the steps. Ben could not tell Sofia what he was searching for.

That night, Ben set his alarm and tried to sleep.

I can't sleep.

He kept having crazy dreams.

Ben's alarm beeped early the next morning.

Ben tiptoed up the attic stairs. This was his last chance to find what he was looking for.

Ben heard extra creaking. Something, or someone, was following him!

What a relief! It was just Sofia.

Ben pulled a piece of string from his pocket.
He tied on a cricket.

That's when Sofia heard the noise. She knew what it was right away.

Sofia picked up her pet snake. She gave it a kiss.

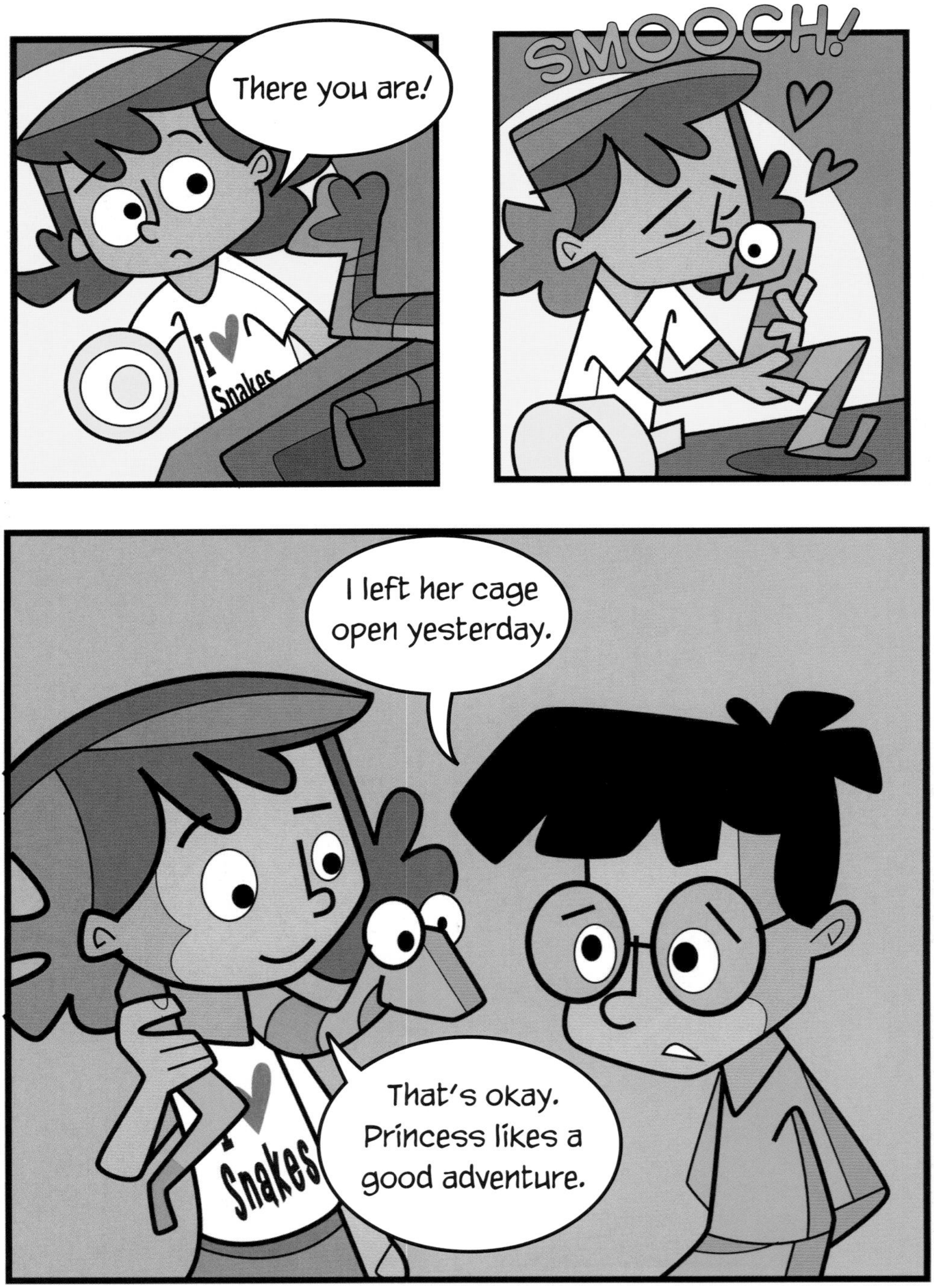
There you are!
SMOOCH!
I left her cage open yesterday.
That's okay. Princess likes a good adventure.
I ♥ Snakes

Ben was glad Sofia wasn't mad. Sofia was glad they found Princess. And Princess was glad to be out of the attic.

ABOUT THE AUTHOR

Cari Meister is the author of many books for children, including the My Pony Jack series and *Luther's Halloween*. She lives on a small farm in Minnesota with her husband, four sons, three horses, one dog, and one cat. Cari enjoys running, snowshoeing, horseback riding, and yoga. She loves to visit libraries and schools.

ABOUT THE ILLUSTRATOR

Artist Rémy Simard began his career as an illustrator in 1980. Today he creates computer-generated illustrations for a large variety of clients. He has also written and illustrated more than 30 children's books in both French and English, including *Monsieur Noir et Blanc*, a finalist for Canada's Governor's Prize. To relax, Rémy likes to race around on his motorcycle. Rémy resides in Montreal with his two sons and a cat named Billy.

GLOSSARY

ALARM (uh-LARM) — an object with a bell or buzzer that wakes people up

ATTIC (AT-ik) — a space in a building just below the roof

COBWEB (KOB-web) — a net of sticky threads made by a spider

CREAK (KREEK) — a loud squeaky noise

TIPTOED (TIP-tohd) — walked very quietly on the tips of the toes

DISCUSSION QUESTIONS

1. Ben is scared to go in the attic. Talk about something that you are scared to do.

2. Why didn't Ben just tell Sofia that he lost Princess? What would you have done?

3. Have you ever lost something that belonged to someone else?

WRITING PROMPTS

1. Ben finds bats in the attic. Make a list of other creatures that could live in the attic.

2. Make a poster describing the missing snake. Be sure to draw a picture and include her name and what she looks like.

3. Ben has strange dreams about bats. Write a few sentences about a strange dream you have had.

THE 1ST STEP INTO GRAPHIC NOVELS

These books are the perfect introduction to the world of safe, appealing graphic novels. Each story uses familiar topics, repeating patterns, and core vocabulary words appropriate for a beginning reader. Combine the entertaining story with comic book panels, exciting action elements, and bright colors and a safe graphic novel is born.

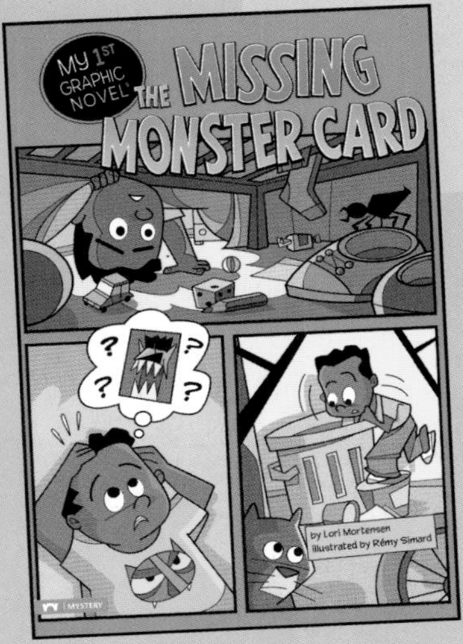
MY 1ST GRAPHIC NOVEL
THE MISSING MONSTER CARD
by Lori Mortensen
illustrated by Rémy Simard
MYSTERY

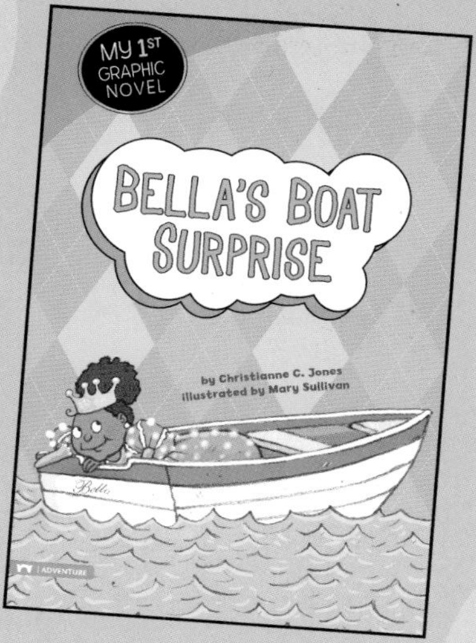
MY 1ST GRAPHIC NOVEL
BELLA'S BOAT SURPRISE
by Christianne C. Jones
illustrated by Mary Sullivan
Bella
ADVENTURE

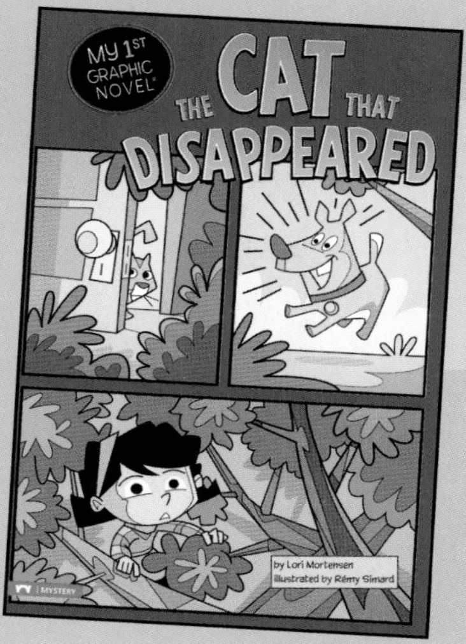
MY 1ST GRAPHIC NOVEL
THE CAT THAT DISAPPEARED
by Lori Mortensen
illustrated by Rémy Simard
MYSTERY

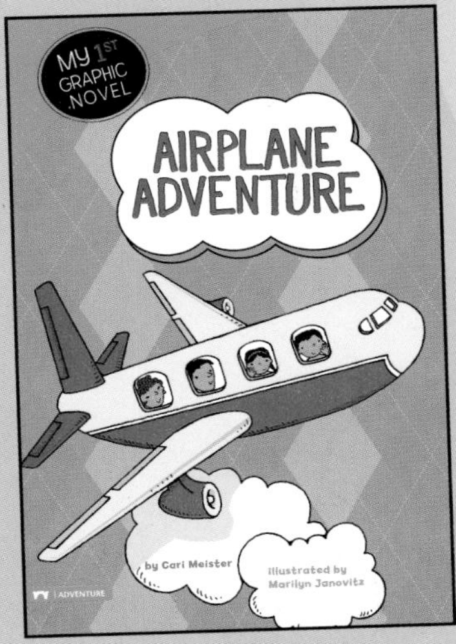
MY 1ST GRAPHIC NOVEL
AIRPLANE ADVENTURE
by Cari Meister
illustrated by Marilyn Janovitz
ADVENTURE

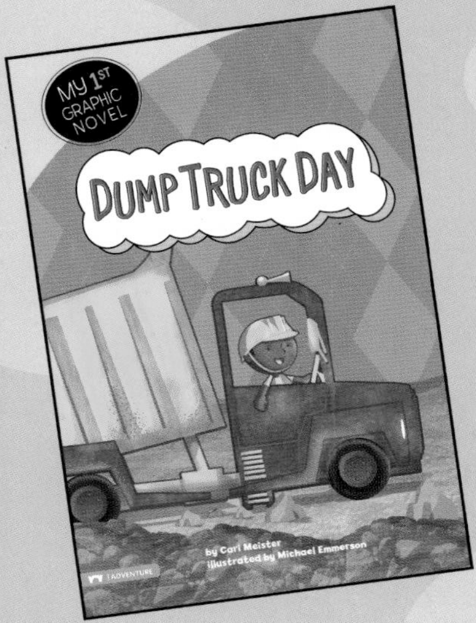
MY 1ST GRAPHIC NOVEL
DUMP TRUCK DAY
by Cari Meister
illustrated by Michael Emmerson
ADVENTURE

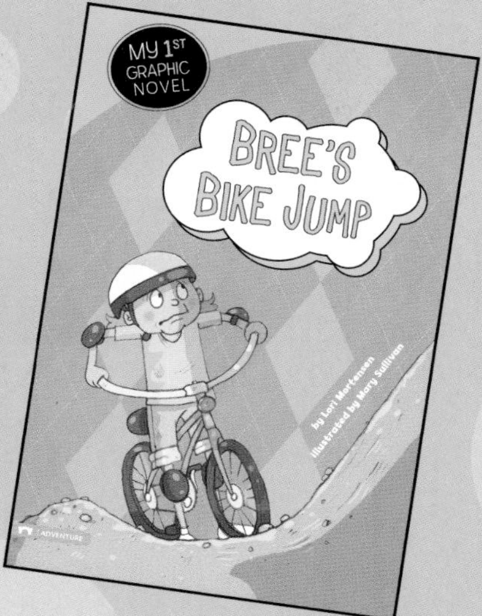
MY 1ST GRAPHIC NOVEL
BREE'S BIKE JUMP
by Lori Mortensen
illustrated by Mary Sullivan
ADVENTURE